# LITTLE PLACE CALLED HOME

# Also by Alexandria Blaelock

SHORT STORY COLLECTIONS
The Haunting of Hayward Hall
Lovelorn, Lovestruck and Love at First Sight
Common or Garden Variety Heroes
Case Files of the Wilkinson National Detective Agency
Unavoidable Fates
Christmas Travesties
Five Faces of Felicia Clarke

FICTION
That Love Nonsense
Taipan vs Brown

MS BLAELOCK'S BOOKS
Stress Free Dinner Parties
Signature Wardrobe Planning
Holistic Personal Finance
Minimally Viable Housekeeping
Planning a Life Worth Living

SELECTED SHORT STORIES

Alma's Grace
Balancing the Book
Best Friends Forever
Christmas Bonanza
Christmas Business
Christmas Conflagration
Christmas Kisses
Fate in Your Hands
Lady of the Looking Glass
Life in the Security Directorate
Long Weekend in the Snow
Love in the Security
Directorate
Love in the Past Tense
Morning Star, Evening Star,
Superstar
Mystery of the Master Suite
Needy Bitch
Payton's Run

Remains of Christmas
Secret Singer
Shining Star
Ship in a Bottle
Simone Says Hands in the Air
Special Relativity in Space
The Bygone Boyfriend
The Day the Schedule Broke
The Ghost Detectors
The Kiss of Death
The Life and Death of
Carmelita Basingstoke
The Mince Pie Mystery
The Palace Hotel
The Pseudonym's Bride
The Shadow Thieves
The Space Time Paradox
Toy Soldiers
Waylon's Way

# LITTLE PLACE CALLED HOME

ALEXANDRIA BLAELOCK

BlueMere Books
MELBOURNE, AUSTRALIA

For permission requests, please contact
enquiries@bluemerebooks.com.

Ordering Information:
Discounts are available on quantity purchases. For details, contact orders@bluemerebooks.com.

Little Place Called Home/Alexandria Blaelock
hardback ISBN: 978-1-922744-20-3
paperback ISBN: 978-1-922744-21-0
digital ISBN: 978-1-922744-22-7

Book Layout © BookDesignTemplates.com
Cover Art © CharactersForYou/depositphotos

# Contents

# INTRODUCTION

"Home is where the heart is," that's what people usually say.

Though it's debatable whether they mean your heart lies with the place or the people you share your living accommodation with.

After all some people loathe their families and prefer to live elsewhere.

Do you and your heart even want the same things?

And how does your heart know where it wants to be, anyway?

I imagine for most of us, that's an easy enough question to answer.

It's the place you grew up in.

The place your memories are; that's where you fell off your bike, that's where you had your first kiss, and that's where the church where you got married.

Perhaps you can trace your family through the streets; that's where Aunty Pauline lives, Great Uncle Henry lives there, and here's the cemetery where seven generations of my family are buried.

The situation is a little harder for some of us.

My parents emigrated when I was young, and I barely remember my life in the "old country".

I visited for a couple of years as a young adult, but it was literally (and figuratively) a foreign country.

I don't know Aunty Pauline, so why would I care where she lives? It's not like she's invited me over or anything.

We moved a lot when I was a child, so you'd need a week's vacation to follow my life around.

My first bike crash is three suburbs away from my first kiss, and they're both on the other side of the country to the place I got married.

We moved so often I can barely remember most of the houses.

I do remember forgetting at least once where I lived and having to find a phone box to call home to get the address.

Terrifying!

And yet, now that I've grown up, it's a funny dinner party story.

And thanks to my father, for whom it was also a funny story, the memory is forever linked with the old English music hall song *Don't Dilly Dally on the Way* by Charles Collins and Fred W. Leigh (1919).

He used to relate the story, and then sing the song, in a ridiculous and overbearing way.

> *My old man said: "Foller the van,*
> *And don't dilly-dally on the way".*

And of course, my parent's friends knew the song too, so they could sing along.

> *Oh! I'm in such a mess.*
> *I don't know the new address -*
> *Don't even know the blessed neighbourhood.*
> *And I feel as if I might*
> *Have to stay out here all night.*

Thankfully, most of my friends don't know the song.

But the place your heart calls to, as it turns out, is far more coincidental and complicated than that.

It starts with the age old debate of city versus country. Inner city or outer city. North or South. East or West.

Sometimes it's about the way the light feels; too bright and harsh, too soft and dim, or just right.

Or the sound of the wind in the trees, or the surf crashing to the beach.

The look of the house, or the smell of the garden.

Perhaps even the quirky mailbox.

This set of literary and fantasy stories, all set in Australia, relate in some way to finding the place your heart wants. A place called home:

- In *Cry in the Darkness* Tom struggles to find his place taming a grant of land.
- While *Millie and the Mountain* shows sometimes the place finds you.
- As Mrs Pearson discovers in *Dream House*, letting go can be harder than you expect..
- Meanwhile, in *Dingo Hunting*, Katie finds a place when she finds a new family.
- While in *Dance of Death*, Li Quan finds his place in the afterlife changes according to where his heart is.

Perhaps being an immigrant has made the search for my place more meaningful.

I chose it.

Or did it choose me?

Alexandria Blaelock
Melbourne, Australia
November, 2022

# ALEXANDRIA BLAELOCK

# CRY IN THE DARKNESS

## A SHORT STORY

# CRY IN THE DARKNESS

The night was breathtakingly hot, close and still.

So dark Tom could barely see an inch in front of him.

The moon was hiding behind the clouds, but here and there a star pierced the gloom with unexpected brightness.

There's too much sky out here.

Trees stretched from horizon to horizon, like an invading army marching relentlessly forward in phalanx formation.

Tucked safely behind their shields, they had no regard for anyone in their way - if you didn't get out of it, they'd mow you down as if you were hay.

There were more creatures than people out here, and in the darkness, they rustled in the bushes.

Their quiet scurrying was an almost continuous assault on Tom's ears, terrifying because he didn't know what they were.

Or whether they ate people.

Or just killed them for fun, and left the remains for scavengers.

You came across half-eaten corpses of things all the time.

He sat on the trunk of a big old gum he'd felled himself with an axe.

It'd taken days, and he had the sore shoulders and blistered hands to prove it.

So torn and blistered he had to wrap them in rags to protect them from the heat of his tin cup and plate.

Even worse, he'd have to do it all again in the morning.

And the next day.

And the one after that.

Tom sighed and leant forward to poke the fire with a stick.

Sparks spattered and flew into the sky.

The oils and resin in the wood popped and flared.

Fires were supposed to be cheerful things.

But Tom had shrunk into himself with pain, fear and defeat. It seemed the surviving eucalypts were leaning menacingly in towards him.

As if they might snatch him up and tear him to pieces in retribution for their fallen comrades.

Fair enough, he supposed.

The pieces he'd stacked up nearby leaked resin. Red, like blood.

Staining the wood as it dripped down to the ground.

When they dried out and were trimmed down, they'd become the walls of his cottage.

Or maybe fence posts, which seemed a demeaning end for a majestic tree that had fought so valiantly to survive.

He was all alone, in wild bushland, with real and supernatural creatures he didn't understand and who didn't understand him.

Lord knows what possessed him to take passage to this inescapably God-forsaken land.

He'd thought there was a fortune to be made.

Though he hadn't reckoned on having to fight nature tooth and nail, day and night, in unrelenting back-breaking, soul-destroying labour.

He was such a dupe.

All very well to have a cheap land grant, but without convict labour to work it, he was on his own.

In fact, he'd be on a boat on his way back to England in an instant, could he only afford the passage.

Everything was wrong here.

The sky too blue, the sun too hot, too many bugs - half of which can kill you.

Too many jumping creatures that move too fast and will break your bones as soon as look at you.

Good eating, though, if you can catch them.

Which is hard because they move too fast and are well used to evasion.

Not enough water, not enough tea, not enough booze, not enough women.

Too many aborigines that either nick your stuff or try to kill you.

Or both.

It was definitely a mistake to come to Australia, even more, to come out here into the bush alone.

But this was his land now, and if he didn't work it, he'd lose it and be left with nothing.

Not even his dignity.

Though right at that moment, Tom wasn't sure his dignity was worth the price.

He could pretty much kiss Mary goodbye.

One or both of them would be dead before he'd established himself sufficiently to ask her to leave London for him.

The last letter he'd received was dated three months ago, and she still seemed keen when she wrote it.

But her parents were keener to get her out of the house; they'd probably sent her into service by now.

Or married her off to John the farrier.

What was wrong with him?

Why did everything he touch turn to shit?

Failed clerk that he was, why, in God's name, did he leave his nice comfortable home in search of adventure?

And why Australia of all places?

Why not America?

Or Canada?

Some other country with a thin edge of civilisation.

Not enough raw wild adventure probably.

Being a bit yellow, New Zealand had been out of the question, but relationships with the Australian aboriginals had definitely been more warlike than he'd imagined.

Tom sighed again.

The one thing to be said for working hard all day was you slept well.

No matter the surface you slept on.

He dusted up the ground a little with his booted foot before rolling out his swag.

Tom wasn't on the track anymore, so he didn't *need* to wrap all his things up in a swag, but he liked to pack it up to keep the bugs out and all his things neat and together.

In this crazy time, you never knew when you'd need to do a runner, whether for the natives, bushrangers, escaped convicts or creatures.

It easier if everything was packed and ready to go, you didn't have to risk sneaking back later to round up your stuff.

He didn't really want to take his boots off for fear of what might move into them, but they needed to air out, as did his feet.

When he put his spares on in the morning, he'd investigate them thoroughly with a stick before they got anywhere near his feet.

He lay on top of the folded blue woollen blanket, protected from the ground by a thick calico base sheet, and rested his head on the lumpy pillowcase containing his spare clothes.

The fire was dying down, sinking into itself as if it too was ashamed of consuming the trees.

Lying on his back, Tom imagined climbing its smoke to heaven, away from this hell.

He was just drifting off to sleep when he thought he heard a scream from the bush, somewhere nearby.

Sleepy and momentarily startled, his first thought was that it was just the start of another nightmare.

Nothing different tonight to any other; no reason to stress, no reason to wake up, no reason to do anything.

But then he heard it again.

He lay, eyes closed, all attention focused on the sounds he was picking up, listening intently for the scream to come again.

Was it real?

Was it a person?

Was it some kind of creature?

Out here, it could be hard to tell.

Possums hissed and snarled at night, but not like that.

And wombats grunted and squealed, but not like that.

This was a noise he hadn't noticed before.

Mind you, if he hadn't visited what passed for the local town a couple of days ago, and caught up with *The Argus* newspaper, he wouldn't have given it a second thought.

He'd have assumed it was some kind of bird or animal and ignored it.

Just rolled over and gone back to sleep.

Or what passes for sleep on stifling hot Summer nights.

But he'd got two newspaper stories stuck in his head and hadn't been able to shake them.

Two stories so typical of life in the colonies.

In the first, Mrs Stevenson had wandered into the bush and disappeared without a trace.

The marriage was rumoured to be an unhappy one. Stevenson was known to be a little too fond of a drink, and some speculated he'd killed his wife.

Perhaps because the alternatives were horrifying.

A gently treated woman alone in the bush, without food or water.

Lost on a hot day, sweating like a pig, walking or running as you looked for a way out, you'd pass out in a matter of hours.

And if you weren't found quickly, you'd probably be dead in a day.

Mind you, it wasn't exactly uncommon for outlying homesteads to be attacked by aborigines or opportunists, and human decency only got a woman alone so far.

As the scream came again, it wasn't hard to imagine some girl or young woman, lost and alone in the bush in her long white nightgown.

Screaming, waiting and listening for some kind of response before screaming again.

Though you had to ask yourself what kind of woman wonders off barefoot in her nightclothes, and whether perhaps she didn't ought to be lost in the bush and die.

Then again, some of them genteel ladies never really got to grips with life in Australia, such as it was.

Some of them were a little more fond of the laudanum bottle than was perhaps proper.

And in their drug-addled states, some of them did some stupid things.

Not that it was any of his business mind, but more a matter for her husband and the priest.

Maybe that was Mrs Stevenson's fate.

The other newspaper story was about some Simms fellow who'd got it in his head that he'd heard a lost child in the bush.

Despite no reports of missing children, they'd got up a search party and searched for days, finding no sign of the child.

The search had been called off, but that guy, haunted by some demon of his own, just wouldn't give up.

He continued searching alone; for days and days and days.

When his horse limped home alone, they went looking for him and found him dead of exhaustion.

The bush'll do that to you.

Turn you around and around, and inside out, and before you know it, you don't know where you are.

Next to no moss on the trees or otherwise to guide you home.

Not that he knew what to look for.

Life in the mean streets of a city does not prepare you adequately for bush life.

The newspapers are full of stories of men getting drunk and getting lost on their way home.

Falling over, passing out, dying of exhaustion.

Let alone those lost explorers dying of exposure after they've already eaten their horses.

Tom heard another scream, maybe a little further away this time.

If it was a woman, why didn't she call "help" or use some other words that would readily identify her as a human in danger?

The desire to be a local hero, lauded in the papers for saving some rich man's wife, warred with the risk of becoming a laughing stock like Simms.

There was a lot of free beer tied up with being a local hero, and not many would say no to that.

Certainly not Tom.

He sat up, scrubbing his eyes, trying to wake up and apply some logic to the situation before he did anything rash.

His grant was 30-acres.

He was surrounded by three other 30-acre grants.

It was about an hour's to ride to his closest neighbour, so it would take about three hours for someone to walk from his nearest neighbour to him.

Perhaps more for a woman on account of her shorter legs.

Maybe an extra hour for a child.

Assuming they followed the road, such as it was, rather than trying to cut through the bush.

And seeing as two of the grants were more or less fenced, there wasn't much point walking through the bush from them.

He only had one neighbour with a wife, and they had a child as well, though Martin was on the un-fenced side.

He was good friends with Martin, so he didn't think Martin would hesitate to come ask him for help with the search.

Because two or more people are going to make a more thorough search than one.

Or at least asking you to turn up at their place in the early morning light to get a good start.

And you see more in the day than the night.

Assuming Martin had noticed he'd lost his wife or daughter at this point.

For that matter, why would Mrs Martin walk cross-country to him anyway?

Surely if they needed his help for some kind of emergency, she'd ride over, not walk.

Tom had no idea where the next closest woman or child was.

Logic suggested the scream was some kind of nocturnal wildlife he'd only noticed because he was on edge about the news articles.

He wriggled around to free the blanket from underneath him and pulled it up to his shoulder as he rolled onto his side.

It was too dark, and the terrain too rough to start looking for a woman who may or may not be lost right now.

But first thing in the morning, he'd ride over to Martin's cottage to be sure.

Hopefully that would be one more strange bush noise he could ignore in the future.


THE END

AUTHOR OF UNAVOIDABLE FATES
ALEXANDRIA BLAELOCK
Millie and the Mountain
A SHORT STORY

# MILLIE AND THE MOUNTAIN

The day we moved into our new home was bright and sunny. Not one of those crisp and cold sunny winter days, but the kind with the soft, warm sunlight that wraps itself around you like a big blanket.

Which was lucky, because the carpets were damp and stinky from whenever the previous owners steam had cleaned them.

How lucky we were to have the doors and windows wide open for long enough to dry the carpets and dissipate the smell before it set in.

And lucky too to have a tiled kitchen big enough to stack all our boxes so they didn't need to wait outside or touch the carpet.

The outside air was tinged with the eucalypt scented woodsmoke drifting lazily across the wire fence from our new neighbour's chimney.

A couple of Magpies clutched the power line as they welcomed us.

Crimson Rosellas peppered us with questions from the naked pear tree.

We were very excited - this was the end of our youthful nomadic existence. It was time to stay in one place and put down a root or two.

For a while anyway.

When we signed the purchase contract, we made a pact to stay there, in that house, at least until the dog we hadn't bought yet died. Say 15 or 20 years.

We were excited about that too.

Not that there's anything wrong with using your employer's greed to travel the world, but in the end, it gets a bit tiresome learning new cultures and languages.

And making new friends only to leave them a couple of years later.

So, we'd tossed a coin, and David's "home" won over mine, and here we were.

Setting up a new home of our own, back in Australia.

Back in the land he'd grown up in, though he'd been away for so long he didn't really know it anymore.

In any case, we hadn't gone back to his sleepy home town; that would have been like getting off an express train while it was still moving.

And we'd chosen Melbourne over Sydney, because it reminded us of the European cities where we'd been happy, rather than the American ones where we hadn't.

Plus, it's not called the Coffee Capital of Australia for nothing!

While we waited for out belongings to arrive, we took a driving holiday round Victoria.

We visited the sandstone ridges and kangaroo mobs of the Grampians, the wide wilderness beaches of Wilson's Promontory, the Goldfields of Ballarat and drove along the Great Ocean Road to Portland.

We were looking for a place we fit.

It's funny, the Australian Aboriginal Nations believe you belong to the land, not the other way around.

That no matter where your people come from, the land you're born on, is your home. And the people who live there, are your people.

That's why it's so important their remains are buried in the land of their people - so their spirits are reborn among their people.

Not that I know a lot about it, but it feels to me, as though the land chooses you.

That it calls and calls until you come to it.

And so it was for us.

We'd gone for a drive through the forests of the Dandenong Ranges National Park.

We'd walked through Mountain Ash trees as tall as City buildings and under ferns almost as tall, drinking in the smell of damp ground and foggy air.

The light streaked through the forest canopy as we held hands, gazing into each other's eyes, standing as still as if we too were deeply rooted in the ground.

All around us wild birds called, and wild creatures rustled in the undergrowth.

We felt the sacred spirit of the land calling us home.

Leaving the Park, we got lost.

And in the best tradition of fairy stories, found ourselves up a dead-end street facing a darling white weatherboard cottage.

It was old, and in bad condition, but it combined all the best features of all the holiday houses we'd visited during our travels.

It was perfect.

When we got back to our rented apartment in the City, we started looking at real estate websites, and wonder of wonders, there was the very same cottage.

Listed that very day.

As if it was meant to be.

Just like the land was calling us home.

We put an offer in the next day, and the day after that, we signed the purchase contract.

The cottage seemed enormous compared to the tiny apartments we'd been living in.

I think you could pretty much fit the one we left in the cottage's lounge.

We didn't know how we'd ever fill it with stuff.

Once we understood how they worked, the large double hung windows, helped cool the house on scorching hot days, as did the copse of gum trees it nestled within.

Not that gum trees are the best for shade, or for the structural integrity of your home, but if you want to live with the sound of birdsong, you have to live in their habitat.

The covered merbau decking was perfect for our new tradition of evening cocktails watching the sunset, and talking about our days.

And when Millie the golden Labrador finally arrived, it was the perfect spot for her to snooze in the morning sunshine or afternoon shade.

Watching the road and waiting for us to come home.

And the mailman.

Labradors have the reputation for hearty appetites, and Millie was no exception. It was a constant struggle to keep her weight down.

One of her favourite treats was possum poo, sucked up as hors d'oeuvres during her morning ablutions.

She also liked fresh fruit, stripped directly from the tree by taking a long run up the yard, launching herself into the air, grabbing a branch in her jaws and letting gravity do its work.

Oddly, after a few half-hearted attempts at catching a bird, she gave up on them.

Perhaps she realised they were good guides to what in the garden might be worth eating at different times of year.

Or perhaps they ganged up on her and introduced her to the consequences of killing their young.

All in all, she was a cheerful and well behaved, if bossy dog.

But, as it turned out, despite our morning walks, she regularly let herself out and took long walks around the neighbourhood on her own.

We only found out when we got home from work one day to find the gates closed, and a note from our neighbour telling us that she'd "rescued" Millie during one of her perambulations.

That night we got out the torches and crawled around in the undergrowth, looking for her escape route with no success.

The next day, our neighbour had contained her in the front garden again, so I put a bucket of water in there for the time after that.

We checked the fence line again, this time shaking it and pulling at the assorted boards, panels and wires it was made up of, but still no sign of her escape route.

Mind you, she was following us around the fence, so perhaps she'd successfully distracted us at the crucial moment.

Clever girl!

But it did mean one of us had to stay home to see how she was escaping, so I negotiated with my boss to work from home for a day.

It turned out to be a very productive day for me, I got a lot done without the day-to-day distractions of telephone calls and useless colleagues.

But, not a successful dog escape detection day.

Millie, had a delightful and restful day indoors sleeping under my desk while I worked.

I kind of liked it, even if it didn't advance the cause.

But it seemed it was enough to turn the corner.

For a while, she was contentedly waiting in the back yard for us when we got home from work.

We thought the situation had been contained.

We were mistaken.

Not that we can blame her.

Dogs are descended from wolves, and wolves roam in packs.

A dog, left on her own all day, is bound to wander looking for something to hang out with.

We started to notice things like leaving a clean dog when we left home in the morning, and finding a filthy one when we got back.

Or that some days she was almost too tired to eat.

Or that she'd be limping.

One Summer evening we got home, and she wasn't there.

We called, and she didn't come.

We kicked her food bowl around the deck, a cue that had always worked in the past, but she didn't come.

Cicadas mocked us from the trees.

We were worried.

Grabbing her lead, we climbed the hill into the National Park, rattling it and calling her name.

It felt like we roamed for miles and miles, for hours and hours, but I'm sure it wasn't that long.

Eventually, we heard her yelp, so we knew she was near.

We kept looking, and finally found her, lying in a large hole nestled in some tree roots.

A half-eaten creature of some kind lay nearby.

She thumped her tail once, and whimpered breathily.

She didn't even try to get up.

She was filthy.

She'd vomited, she'd lost control of her bowels, and she was lying in it.

We thought she'd probably eaten the creature. And that it was either decomposing or had died from some kind of poison.

Regardless, it'd made her ill and we had to get her to the vet as quickly as possible.

David is fitter than me, and has longer legs, so he bolted back to the house to get the car and a blanket.

I collected the dead creature in a poo bag in case the vet wanted to test it or something.

Hoping she could walk, I tried to roll Millie out of the hole and onto her feet, but just succeeded in rolling her over.

She didn't have the strength or inclination to get to her feet and walk.

Her healthy appetite meant her 33 kg body was too heavy for me to lift, if I was going to move her, I had no option but to drag her.

Across the stony ridge and down the hill towards the closest place we could meet David and the car.

Snagging her body here and there on tree stumps and branches.

Would we get to the vet any quicker?

Maybe a little.

Would she be better or worse off with road rash as well as poisoning?

I was afraid worse, but I couldn't just sit and wait for David to return.

Deciding my t-shirt would offer Millie some protection, I took it off and started wrapping it around her body.

She whined as I manhandled it underneath her and tied the sleeves across her chest.

Then I grabbed her front legs and start pulling her towards me.

She was fine for a little while, but soon enough she was trying to pull free of me.

We rested for a bit, and then we were off again.

It seemed like forever before David arrived with the blanket.

We wrapped her up like a sausage and carried her to the car.

David took off for the vet with a squeal of tyres.

I'd forgotten I wasn't wearing a top until we rushed into the surgery, and the waiting pet owners looked at us curiously.

The vet nurse kindly gave me a scrub top to wear.

We sat on the hard seat waiting for a vet to see us, cradling Millie on our laps, stroking her head and patting her swaddled belly.

She wasn't chafing at the restraint, and we thought for sure she was a gonner.

They took Millie away to see to her, and we waited, even though they told us not to.

Taking it in turns to pace up and down the waiting room, even though they'd told us to go home.

Stinking up the place and getting in people's way, even though they said they'd call as soon as they knew anything at all.

Waiting as the sun set.

Waiting while the nurses gossiped, smelling their dinners, and until our bums lost all feeling.

We waited, and waited.

And then waited some more.

A burst of light, and noise, and movement, and we were in the recovery room with Millie.

She was clean, sedated, and hooked up to a drip.

She was going to live.

It seemed as though the land had claimed her too, and kept her safe within its soil until we could collect her.

While she was in dog hospital, we had all the fences replaced so she couldn't escape again.

And once she'd recovered, we took her to a local dog shelter to choose a new friend she could stay home with.

Now she's always on the deck waiting for us when we get home.


THE END

# ALEXANDRIA BLAELOCK

# DREAM HOUSE

## A SHORT STORY

# DREAM HOUSE

Bill kicked the stand of his red postie motor-cycle out, and let the bike lean on the rest. He took his helmet off and placed it in the mail-bag attached to the handlebars before scratching his head and ruffling his hair with both hands to help the sweat evaporate.

He paused for a moment to enjoy the stillness in his body.

Without removing his sunglasses, turned his face towards the sun, closed his eyes and took a deep breath of the fresh gum scented air.

Then he stood and lifted his leg over the bike and placing his hands on the small of his back, leaned back, folding his shoulders out to stretch out his chest.

That was a bit better.

Intertwining his arms and pushing them out, he leaned forward to stretch his back and shoulders. Then rocked his head from side to side stretching out his neck as he ripped open his jacket and flapped it to get a breeze through his sweaty shirt.

Having eased his tense body, he pulled a stainless steel water flask from the bike's saddlebag, and took a swig, swishing it around his dry mouth before swallowing.

The water always tasted better when he hit the old part of the suburb.

And one day, when he could afford it, he wanted to buy a house around here.

And if he could have his pick, it would be old Mrs Pearson's - number 17 Mason Close.

A beautiful, old, Federation style, white weatherboard cottage with a heritage red steel roof, on a big block half-way up a hill in a quiet cul-de-sac.

With highly scented yellow David Austin roses in the front garden and gum trees in the back.

Bluestone chip driveway and white picket fence.

Throw in the wicker porch setting, and you've got yourself a deal.

He signed and leaned on the green mail distribution box, taking another drink from his flask.

The gum tree the box was under didn't cast much shade, but the smell of it made this the best place to take a moment to rest on his entire delivery run.

Plus, magpies roosted in it, and he loved listening to their melodic conversations.

A young-un settled in a branch close by and looked at him intently. He pulled a small snack from his pocket, and the bird snatched it from his hand and flew higher up into the tree.

Bill knew he shouldn't feed the thing, but there was swooping season to think about.

While his neck drape protected him from the sun and rain, it wasn't so useful when swooping season came around.

He knew the magpies had chased off the postie before him, and he wanted to stay on their good side!

He checked the time, then fastened his water bottle.

He unlocked the box, took out the pre-sorted mail and quickly sorted some in the front bag, and the rest in the saddlebags. Resealed the Velcro on his jacket, fastened his helmet and he was ready to go again.

The first section of Tuesday's delivery run was uneventful. While email slowed down the letters, it meant more small packages, but that day, there wasn't much to deliver.

Perhaps that's why the bike's brakes still squeaked annoyingly every time he slowed.

Not enough money to fix them properly, or maintain spares, or whatever.

Maybe he was 16th in the queue, just like the library waiting list for the latest Grisham novel.

Fortunately, nothing for 10 Grant Street, so the terrier had to content itself with running along the fence, barking like a demon-possessed dog as he sped past.

Tempting as it was, he did not make a face or raise any fingers in the dog's direction.

Nearly wiped out by a delivery van reversing out of 52 Moore Street without looking. Or tooting their horn. Though to be fair, the delivery drivers had their own issues to deal with.

And then nearly run off the road by a car coming round the roundabout at the other end. Not looking, not giving way, too busy thinking they were too important to consider the needs of any other road users.

Just like all the others.

Though it did make delivering mail a more exciting career than it might otherwise seem.

Had to slow down and weave in and out of badly placed rubbish bins in Clementine Avenue. Honestly, it's not like Council didn't have guidelines about that. Hopefully, the ones recommended by the Corporation.

Almost drove into an enormous pothole on Erica Avenue. It'd been there for weeks, so you'd think by now he'd have habituated the out-swing to avoid it. He wondered how much longer before they fixed it. Maybe they were going to wait until the current round of roadworks were complete so they could dig it all up again.

Around the corner into Bridge Road and collided with a pile of prunings stacked up waiting for collection. It might be hot, but thank goodness for the heavy-duty protective gear. Bill quietly but firmly cursed as he hauled himself upright and dragged the bike back out of the mess.

Kicking what was left of the stack for good measure and leaving it for the resident to sort out.

He walked the bike the length of one house and garden to make sure it was fine to keep riding, before propping it up and walking back to take a couple of photos of the mess. He tapped out an Incident Notification Form, attached the pictures and sent them into Head Office.

The stack was probably a bit high for the guys who'd be coming out to take the prunings away anyway. He'd probably done them a favour collapsing it down a bit.

A package to deliver at 75 Spencer Street, so he propped the bike and walked to the door. Rang the doorbell, and after a beat or two, knocked on the door as well. No answer.

Double checked the address to make sure it was the right house, then left it by the door, trying to make sure it wasn't visible from the street. Took a photo, sent it back to Head Office as proof of delivery.

Paused to scratch the head of a calico cat sunning itself on the porch on the way back to his bike.

All in all, just another day delivering the mail.

Rain, hail or shine.

Or as the Corporation expressed it, "committed to providing trusted, relevant and reliable services."

Load of Marketing BS if you asked him.

And if you asked, he'd have to be honest and say that as usual, he was trying to make up a bit of time so he could slow down and enjoy the ride along Mason Close.

He paused at the bottom of the street and looked up the tree-lined road to the top of the hill.

Something about all those trees, clustered in small arboreal communities, as if they were slowly migrating downhill was relaxing.

Maybe the Japanese were onto something with the whole forest bathing thing.

It was certainly way more restful than looking along his street at all the tower apartment buildings.

More sun and air for one thing.

More green for another.

Less graffiti, less rubbish and less gang culture.

He cruised slowly up the street, slowing here and there to lean the bike and stuff letters in mailboxes.

Or behind the fence and on top of the box.

That wasn't really fair, there was no gang culture where he lived.

It was just a bunch of kids with nothing better to do. Sooner he got his out of there, the better.

He put number 32's mail back in the bag because they still hadn't replaced their mailbox.

He'd tucked a notice in the door a week ago telling them the mail would be stored at the local post office for seven days before being returned to sender until a new box was installed.

The place looked a bit unkempt, and he wondered if anyone still lived there.

Reaching the top of Mason Close, he paused and looked back down. From this angle, steep enough to be slightly vertiginous.

During school holidays, the space was crowded with kids who plodded up the hill pushing bicycles or carrying skateboards so they could coast back down.

And it was something he knew his kids would love to do as well.

Hell, some days, he enjoyed the coast down too.

Always slowing down to take in the full glory of number 17.

It was amazing how the view changed so much from day to day.

Today, there seemed to be a pile of filthy old clothing abandoned in the front garden.

Bill was a couple of houses down when it occurred to him that perhaps the pile of old clothes was actually Mrs Pearson, who was becoming increasingly frail.

It wasn't any of his business, but she was a charming lady, always ready to a chat if she was in the garden when he dropped the mail off.

And always offered him a cold drink when he delivered a package.

He couldn't just drive on without checking.

It was going to be a scorching hot day, and if she'd fallen, and couldn't get up, she might not last the day.

He turned back.

It *was* Mrs Pearson. Face down on the front lawn

Bill scanned the area and saw no obvious hazards so he got off the bike and headed towards her.

"Mrs Pearson, are you all right?" he asked.

She didn't move, or say anything.

"Mrs Pearson?" he asked, kneeling beside her and giving her shoulder a little shake.

Still no response.

He ripped his gloves off and gently rolled her on her back, tilting her head back and lifting her chin.

Bill turned his head and listened for breathing while he watched her chest and saw the faintest sign of movement.

Thank goodness.

A quick check of her clothes found no blood, and while her arms and legs were that peculiar, papery bluey white that elderly people's skin is prone to be, didn't seem to be cut or bitten.

Bill exhaled in a relieved whoosh.

He bent her closest arm upwards at the elbow, making sure her palm was facing up, then brought her other arm across her chest, resting the back of her hand against her cheek.

He found the leg furthest from him, and pulled it up through a fistful of skirts, so her foot was flat on the ground, then holding her knee and the hand on her cheek, rolled her body towards him, easing her into the recovery position.

Then tilted her head so her airway stayed open, propping it up with the hand on her cheek while he called for an ambulance.

Every five minutes or so, he called her name so see if she was responsive, then put his head close to hers to check she was still breathing.

Bill was about to roll her onto her other side when the ambulance finally arrived, and he could step back to let the ambos take over.

As they prepared to take her away, he gave them his contact number, just in case.

And as he watched them drive away, hoped she was going to be okay.

He filled out another incident form and sent it to Head Office.

He had no idea whether Mrs Pearson had family nearby or not, but he wrote a note on a Failure to Deliver Card and left it in the mailbox.

Just in case.

The rest of his run passed in a daze and the first thing he did when he got home was open a beer and sit out on the tiny balcony of his flat to drink it.

And a couple more after that.

It was such awful bad luck.

When he checked the next day, his note was still there. And the day after that, and the day after that. And the same the following Monday too. So, he stopped checking.

«« • »»

A few weeks later, she was sitting on the porch, and he had the idea she was waiting for him.

He rode up the drive and got off the bike to talk to her.

"Lemonade?" She offered, "homemade?"

"I shouldn't, but yes. Thank you."

She filled a glass with the bitter, slightly sweet, pale yellow liquid.

"It seems I should thank you. I'm told, if not for you, I would have died."

He nodded his head, just once.

She sighed. "At my age, living is not always the best option."

"I'm sorry."

"Not your fault lad," she patted his leg, "it's just the nature of life.

But I have no family, so now I have to sell the house and move into a nursing home to get "proper" care."

"I'll buy it," he blurted.

"I beg your pardon?"

"I'm sorry. I suppose you'd call me forward. But I want to buy your house."

The old woman smiled a little, "yes, I suppose I would call you forward. But why do you want to buy the house?"

"Because it's beautiful."

"It is that on the outside, but I'm an old woman, it might be different on the inside."

"I imagine it might be a bit old-fashioned on the inside, and maybe a bit worn down and a bit behind on the maintenance, but anyone who looks as neat and elegant as you, and takes such good care of their garden is probably not going to let things go in the house."

"Things have run down a little since my Bill died, but I do my best."

"Was that your husband's name? Bill."

"Yes, William Garrett Pearson. He had a heart attack and died a few years ago."

Bill snorted, "that's odd, my name is William Grant Peterson."

"That is rather curious. Would you like to see the inside?"

"I would love to."

Mrs Pearson leveraged herself out of her chair with a walking stick topped with a crystal knob and opened the screen door for him.

He stepped inside and waited for her.

She poked him with the walking stick, "don't wait for me boy, go have a look round."

"Yes, Miss Havisham," the words were out of his mouth before he could stop them.

Fortunately, she snorted and tapped the stick on the ground.

"Miss Havisham indeed. I'll wait outside," she said, letting the door swing closed in his face as she turned back to her seat.

Bill walked from room to room in awe.

Even though the last time it had been updated was clearly the fifties, the interior was immaculate.

His mother's home had been stuffed full of junk when she passed away, with next to nothing salvageable let alone saleable.

He and his sister had filled three of the big skips with rubbish, and by the time they'd paid for all that, there was just enough money left in the estate to go out for dinner.

By contrast, Mrs Pearson's home was austere. Each room held a simple suite of furniture, and one significant piece of art, whether canvas, sculpture or ceramic.

Three bedrooms and one bathroom might be considered small by most, but the ceilings were high and rooms a good size, especially with so little furniture.

And with the curtains closed over the slightly ajar double-hung windows, the rooms were dim and cool, so the lack of air conditioning might not be a problem.

Unlike his tiny flat, exposed to the sun throughout the Summer.

Out the back, a verandah ran the full length of the house, shading it from the sun. Providing a comfortable vantage point to enjoy the garden, a sort of natural native landscape.

There was plenty of room to move.

To breath.

To take up space.

He had no trouble imagining his family eating in the dining room, queueing up for the toilet, having barbecues on the verandah.

Bill wanted the house more than he'd wanted his wife.

And he'd wanted her a lot.

But he had to be fair to Mrs Pearson.

He had to pay her market price, and he wasn't entirely sure he could afford that.

"Well?" she asked when he returned to the front porch.

He opened his mouth, but no words came out, so he shrugged his shoulders.

She smiled, "I know. I felt the same when I first saw her too."

"Her?"

"Her. The garden was full of Marguerite Daisies that day, so we started calling the house Marguerite."

"Suits her."

"Indeed," she said, leaning back in her chair, "we bought her not long after we married. I'll miss her, but she's not the same without him."

She wiped a tear from her eye.

"Right. I'll get three market appraisals, and we can talk some more when we see what they come back as. Deal?"

"Deal," he said.

She spat in her hand and held it out for him to shake. He looked at it for a moment, then spat in his own and clasped hers in both of his.

He hadn't made a commitment to do more than talk about it further, but he hoped his wife would forgive him.

«« • »»

Several weeks later, he saw Mrs Pearson on the porch, waiting for him.

He pulled in, walked her mail up to her, and accepted her invitation to sit and take some lemonade.

He sat on the edge of the chair.

"Your wife's a lovely young thing, isn't she?"

"When did you meet Sandra?"

"She popped out to say hello, and take a look at the house a week or two ago."

"She didn't tell me that!"

"Why would she Bill?"

"Well... Um... Ah..."

Mrs Pearson sipped some lemonade, "she loved the house, you know."

Bill relaxed a little, and gulped half his glass.

"Let's move on," she handed him some folded pages, "here are the quotes."

He flicked through the pages, outrage warring with relief."

"Surely this is not enough for the property."

"Apparently everyone's looking for four bedrooms and at least two bathrooms these days. All the agents I spoke to said I'd be lucky if I even got land value because the house would probably be knocked down by the new owner."

"Sacrilege!"

"I know, but there you have it."

"I promise I won't knock Marguerite down."

"I think she knows it too.

"Now. What say we go with the highest quote and I'll throw in the furniture and most of the other bits and pieces."

"That's not enough Mrs Pearson, and what will you use yourself?"

She grimaced as she nodded at the house, "I have to make do with their cheap and nasty furniture, and they're quite prescriptive about what I can take, which is next to nothing."

"Well, yes, but—"

"And quite simply, I can't be bothered making any arrangements to get rid of it all."

"Oh. Ah. Okay then."

She handed him another set of papers, "I bought a sales contract from the newsagent, and I've filled all the bits in. Why don't you take it home to Sandra, and pop back tomorrow to let me know what you're going to do."

«« • »»

It seemed like no time at all before the bright sunny morning of moving day arrived. The loan had gone through without a hitch, the deposit paid, bags and boxes packed and on the truck.

The family piled in the car, with a big bunch of flowers and some homemade ANZAC cookies for Mrs Pearson.

She greeted them with kisses and held the door open for the kids to run through, shrieking at each other, and out the back to the verandah before running back in shouting about a picnic.

Mrs Pearson left her small suitcase by the door and took them out to the verandah and the little picnic she'd set up.

Champagne on ice for the adults, and fizzy drinks for the kids.

A Victoria sponge, cucumber sandwiches, fresh strawberries with sweetened cream and potato chips.

She poured drinks for the kids, then the Champagne for the adults. Holding her glass up as a toast, she said, "I hope you'll be as happy here as Bill and I were."

"And we hope you'll be happy too," Bill replied.

Mrs Pearson snorted, but said, "cheers" and sipped the wine.

The doorbell rang.

"That'll be your movers," she said, "you go sort it out, and I'll watch the kids."

"They're a bit of a handful, are you sure you'll be okay?"

Mrs Pearson gestured at them halfway up a tree, "I'm pretty sure they'll be fine a while longer."

Bill nodded and want back in the house.

"Thanks so much," Sandra said, and chased after him.

It took nearly an hour for the movers to unpack the truck and stack all their belongings in the dining room and leave.

Bill and Sandra went back out the back and saw Mrs Pearson had slumped a little in her chair, her chin resting on her chest.

He made a step towards her, but Sandra put out a hand to stop her.

"Leave her. She's fallen asleep, let her rest a little longer. It's going to be hard for her to leave the house she spent her entire married life in."

Bill patted his wife's hand and smiled down at her. "I hope our marriage is as long and happy as hers."

She wrinkled her nose as she smiled back, "me too."

They left her a little longer while they worked in the kitchen together to make a thick, spicy vegetable soup for lunch to go with the fresh bread rolls they'd bought on the way.

Mrs Pearson was a little embarrassed to be woken but enjoyed her lunch.

Bill and Sandra took the kids for a walk around the neighbourhood to give Mrs Pearson a chance to say goodbye to her home, and when they got back, she'd gone.

Bill felt the house was sad to see her go, so he patted the hallway door frame as he passed through into the kitchen, "Don't worry Marguerite," he told it, "we're here for you."

His wife and children laughed at him, but they all patted the hallway door frame on their way through too.

That evening, after the kids had gone to bed, Bill and Sandra sat together on a bench on the back verandah, holding hands and enjoying the sunset.

"Do you think houses have souls?" he asked his wife.

"Of course," she replied, "I think owners leave a little piece of theirs behind when they go."

"Mmmm," said Bill, "I think this is a happy house."

She squeezed his hand, "Yes. We're lucky. It's a house people keep for a long time."

"I'm so glad to get out of that flat."

"We'll be happier here, I'm sure."

He squeezed her hand, "I know we will."

**THE END**

AUTHOR OF UNAVOIDABLE FATES

# ALEXANDRIA BLAELOCK

# DINGO HUNTING

A SHORT STORY

# DINGO HUNTING

Steve led the way up the embankment, because, well, Steve always did.

Something about his wild blond surfer hair (hundreds of kilometres from the sea) and his deep ocean blue eyes just inspired the others to follow him regardless of the consequences.

That was how Jimmy lost a finger in the combine harvester accident, though you can't really say it was an accident when we all knew the risks.

Jimmy just wasn't fast enough that time.

We called it the embankment, but it was a natural phenomenon. We had no idea whether it was an ancient caldera, cenote or maybe even a meteor strike.

But there was a steep climb up, followed by a quick, squealing stumble down through the red dirt, and you were in the perfect place for teenage hijinks.

The basin was so large you almost couldn't see the other side of it. The slopes were covered in a sparse layer of scrub that thickened as you reached the bottom, so you had to fight your way into the centre of the depression.

The bushes were dry and scratchy, and one time Scarlet cut her shoulder open and needed twenty-five stitches to close it back up.

So, every now and then we'd borrow a couple of chainsaws and hack a winding path through to the centre.

For some reason, we thought a winding path would be less obvious to outsiders than a straight one.

And it did make arriving at the centre seem much more like a journey.

The centre held a mysterious stone circle that needed a particular kind of approach, and a nice straight, broad avenue just wasn't the way to do it.

The circle wasn't like a Stonehenge kind circle, all nice and neat and precise.

It was just a bunch of large rocks, but when you looked at them from the right angle, they looked exactly like a circle of snarling dingo teeth rising from the ground.

Like some monstrous beast had been caught just before it manifested and was now stuck forever with just its snout poking out of the ground.

And when the wind came in from just the right direction, you could almost believe it was whining and begging to be set free.

And of course, the path we made was as if you'd walked up its throat and out its mouth, so it seemed like you'd crossed a mystical portal into another world.

Naturally, best at night in the flickering light of a fire made with collected scrub branches.

And even better with a few stolen beers and a couple of joints.

The place had always inspired rumours about lost and stolen children - the kids who were too slow to get away from the faeries, but what modern kid believes in them anymore?

Especially in the outback of Australia.

When faeries remained back in assorted old countries, and anyway, they couldn't survive in the bright, direct, desert sunlight, could they?

Never did we think there was any truth to those rumours.

If, in fact, there were any missing kids at all, we thought they'd just packed up their swag and run off to the big smoke.

Like we all wanted to.

Though maybe only Steve really did, while we just said we did for bravado's sake.

So.

Steve had a thing for pretty, dark-haired Katie, and we all knew she didn't really like him at all.

But kids are kids, and Steve was Steve, and Katie didn't really have a choice in the matter.

Katie belonged to Steve for as long as he wanted her, and when it got difficult, we just kind of slunk away so we wouldn't be tempted to do anything stupid.

Poor Katie.

That night, Steve paused at the top of the embankment for a moment, silhouetted by the full moon before rushing down the other side.

Someone else had got there first.

We could see the glow of their fire, smell their barbecued meat and hear their deep drunken laughter.

Steve was ropable, and we all kind of stepped back out of his way while he told us what he was going to do with the intruders, and how we were going to help.

Steve talked a good game, but we were kids, and they sounded like men, and most likely, we didn't have a hope in hell of doing what Steve wanted.

So while Steve delivered a rousing and inciting speech to his assembled troops, most of them took the opportunity to do a runner before things kicked off.

I didn't have any intention of getting involved, but this time, I was the one not fast enough.

He collared me and pushed me ahead of the rest, so I stumbled out the dingo's jaws into a roar of grown-up laughter.

They were tall, well-built guys with longish black hair. But they looked like bad guys to me, leather pants and tatts and stuff, like a bikie gang.

The leader's dark pants were tucked into his long boots, and his scratched and scarred, dark leather vest hung loose and open.

His bare chest and arms were covered in tattoos, and in the flames, they seemed to writhe across his body in torment.

His black eyes were outlined in Kohl, and as his gaze glanced off me, I was so afraid I tripped over my feet and wet my keks as I fell.

I slithered the hell out of the way as fast as I could.

He rested his hands low on his hips as he cocked his head to look Steve up and down. Katie was a step behind Steve, and he was holding her by the wrist so she couldn't get away.

The leader smiled a little as he walked around the pair.

Steve kind of leant away from him, and Katie kind of leaned towards him.

The fire cast his face into light and shade, outlining his hook nose and glinting off the silver crown-like thing that held his top knot in place.

He pulled Katie towards him, and I don't know if Steve was surprised or recognised a superior force, but he let go of her.

The guy spread his legs a little and pushed his hands up under her skirt. He cupped her under the bum as he held her close, pressed his face into the crook of her neck, and breathed in deeply.

Then he kind of growled, bent her backwards and forced a kiss on her lips.

A long, slow, deep, thorough kiss.

I thought Steve'd go mental, but he took a step back, away from the pair.

"I'll let you go if you leave her behind," the guy said.

Steve turned, and without a word, ran back down the dingo's throat.

I danced around a bit, backwards and forwards, half a mind to do the same.

But I wasn't going to leave Katie there on her own, so I darted forwards and punched the guy in the back.

He laughed.

I got a bit mad and went for him again, but he turned and flicked me in the middle of my forehead with his middle finger like I was a bug on his shoulder and I don't remember anything after that.

«« • »»

The next morning, when Katie woke me up, I was still inside the embankment, but there was no sign of the bikies.

I had the mother of all hangovers.

She helped me up, draped me over her shoulder and helped me scramble over the embankment.

"What happened?" I asked.

"What do you remember?"

I wasn't above a bit of exaggeration, "nothing after that guy hit me."

"What guy?"

"You know, the bikie guy."

"There wasn't a guy. We just got drunk and told scary stories."

"Well, where are all the others then?"

"You wandered off and got lost. I got worried and came back early for you."

I didn't point out any of the holes in her story, like the adult size boot prints.

Or the chewed-up bones.

Or that she was wearing the same clothes, and they were filthy

Or what I later found out was a fingernail-sized bruise on my forehead.

When I got home, I was in so much trouble I was grounded for a month, and my parents set me to fencing, checking and maintaining the pumps, pipes and dam banks, and cleaning out the milking sheds and machinery.

When the cops came round asking after Steve, I wanted to protect Katie, so I told them her story.

That I got drunk and passed out early.

He was there at the start, and he was gone when I work up.

I didn't mention the bikie gang.

I saw Katie and the others at Church, but no one knew where he was.

We agreed he must have packed up and run away to Melbourne.

Doubt anyone else believed it either, but without a body, what were the other options?

We never went back to the embankment.

The years went by, and Steve's folks sold up the farm and moved away.

His missing-persons poster faded and went brown, the edges curled up in the heat, and he was forgotten.

Katie went away to study graphic design, and I took over the farm when my parents moved to the seaside.

It was like Steve had never even existed, except, maybe, as a scary story for the next generation to take over the embankment.

After a bit, Katie's Mum got sick, and she came home to take care of things.

She had an online business with customers all over the place and said it didn't make any difference to her whether she worked from home or the City.

We hooked up.

One night, as she reached over to haul herself out of bed, I noticed a burn on her left shoulder blade.

Something about the way she moved made it look like a dingo howling.

When I asked her about it, she tried to pretend it wasn't there.

And after I traced its outline on her back, that it was something else.

But I reminded her I was the last one there the night Steve disappeared.

She looked over her shoulder at me, shaking her head a little so her long black hair fell back and concealed the mark.

I reached out to brush it aside so I could inspect the mark closely, but something in her eyes made me put my hand back down.

She looked at me for a long time, then got up, pulled her hair aside and placed herself in front of the mirror where she could see the dingo clearly.

It was all done so smoothly it was clear she'd done it a billion times before.

She reached behind her back and touched the mark.

From where I lay, it looked like she was stroking its chin.

"I made a deal," she said.

The moon went behind a cloud, casting her face into shadow, but I swear the dingo on her back yawned, and a faint red glow rose in her eyes.

And then the moon came out, and she threw herself back on the bed beside me, leaning on an elbow, absently stroking my chest as she thought about what to say.

"Most men think the pack leader is the alpha male, but they're wrong," she smiled down at me, one of her canines caught on her lip.

"The leader is the alpha female. It's only by her leave that her lieutenant decides what to hunt, where to eat, when to sleep and mate with her.

"And clearly, the best leader is young, strong and determined."

She was looking past me, out the window, towards the embankment in the distance.

"Someone cunning, who can control the worst tendencies of the pack, and drive them down the path they need to go."

She flicked one of my nipples with her middle finger, and I gasped, unsure whether to cover it or tough it out.

"She's the mother of the pack. Dogs learn their places while they're at her teats. Those with a fighting spirit take their places at front and scout the way, others wait their turn and protect the rear. But they *all* obey their mother.

"Sometimes, a pack loses its mother. They'll carry on for a time, but without a new mother, they're lost, without direction. Sometimes, a pack like that tears itself apart.

"And when we met that pack on the embankment, I realised it was missing its mother."

"But they weren't dogs, they were bikies."

"Were they? What gives you that idea?"

"Well, they were big hairy guys in leather."

"Were they?"

"Well, maybe they weren't bikies, but they were definitely guys."

"Are you sure?"

"Okay, I wasn't conscious for long, but they sure looked like guys."

"They did look like guys, but they were elemental dingoes, in the form of humans."

I thought she was making fun of me, so I leaned towards her, intending to sit up and get out of bed in a huff.

She laid her palm on my chest, and no matter how hard I tried, I wasn't strong enough to sit up past that point.

"I thought you wanted to hear the story."

"I wanted the truth, and in this day and age that doesn't include spirit creatures."

She smiled and moved her hand.

I was still straining to sit up, so I rocketed up, through the place where she'd been sitting and fell on the floor.

Hard.

I looked around for her, and she was on the other side of the room, half-dressed already.

"Katie, what's going on?"

She paused as she pulled on her t-shirt, "There are more things in heaven and earth, Horatio, than are dreamt of in your philosophy." she quoted.

"But Katie—"

"Call me when you really want to know."

She walked out the door, and by the time I'd disentangled myself from the sheets and run, naked, out to the verandah, she was gone.

No sign that she'd even been there, save maybe, for a drift of dust in the light breeze.

«« • »»

So she'd got my goat up with that bloody dog story, though given her Mum was a breeder she'd know all that stuff.

But elementals for god's sake.

She'd be telling me the bikie gang were were-dingoes next.

I stamped about the farm, milking cows, and getting more and more annoyed as the days went by.

And then, I don't know why, but I started watching the animals.

The milking herd follows a clear daily routine in and out of the milking sheds twice a day, but I noticed it was the same old cow that got the herd moving.

We don't use many dogs, because it's in a cow's best interest to get into the milking shed, but I noticed my bitch Blue yipping at the others, keeping the pack in line.

Was there a nugget of truth in the elemental story?

I decided to visit the embankment.

And I was a little afraid, so I took Blue with me.

I parked the ute in the flat space by the road we used to park our pushbikes, though threw them is a more accurate description.

Blue leapt out of the tray almost before I'd pulled the handbrake, and was off up the rise before I'd got one foot on the ground.

I confess I dithered, afraid both of what I might find, and what I might not.

The scrub was wild enough that I thought no one had visited for years, but the town's dying what with the drought and low milk prices.

I pushed my way further and further in, and all of a sudden, I broke into the centre.

Only it wasn't the centre, the stone circle was missing, and I was looking up at the other side.

So, I climbed up and looked back across the basin, and all I could see was dense bush.

No paths, no stones, no gaps.

Blue yipped from somewhere, and I whistled, and in a few seconds, she came bounding up the rise to meet me.

So that was that.

I called Katie.

«« • »»

It was a hot day, a few days after her mother's funeral, when we met at the local footy ground.

I went to kiss her, but she twisted out of my grasp.

And I guess that was fair enough.

"I'm sorry about your Mum Katie."

She grimaced, "what do you want Mike?"

"I went to the embankment, and the stones are gone."

"So?"

"I want to know about the elementals."

She rolled her eyes at me, "It was just a story, I was winding you up."

"I don't believe you."

She shrugged and turned away as if she was looking for someone "not my problem."

I could see through the armhole of her tank top, and I thought maybe the dingo scar was gone from her shoulder.

I wondered for a moment if I'd imagined the whole thing.

She waved at a guy who walked onto the pitch.

"I've got to go Mike," she said, "I'm leaving town today, and my lift's just arrived."

He was a tall, well-built guy with short black hair. His blue button-down shirt was tucked into his jeans, but the sleeves were rolled up to his forearms.

When he saw her, he opened his arms, and as his sleeves pulled up, I thought I saw the flash of coloured tatts.

She jogged across to him, leaping the last step into his embrace.

He swung her around, and I thought I recognised his hook-nosed profile from somewhere but I couldn't say where.

That was the last time I saw Katie.

But now and again, when I hear a wild dog, or maybe a dingo howling, or see one silhouetted on the horizon, I wonder if it's her.

THE END

# ALEXANDRIA BLAELOCK

# DANCE
## OF
# DEATH

A SHORT STORY

# DANCE OF DEATH

Death looked down the listless dry street. The sun-bleached wood of the run-down buildings was almost as white as his bones and just as glary in the sun.

What remained of the roofs were grey with lichen.

A solitary street lamp marking the coach stop leaned drunkenly on its post.

The town was as parched and dry as him.

Leaning on his scythe, he reached into his heavy black wool cowl and pulled out a plain, but serviceable wooden hourglass and held it up to his skeletal face.

Surely it was later than that?

He gave it a vigorous shake, but the build-up of sand didn't change or move any faster.

A light breeze wrapped his cowl around his legs as it lifted the red dust from one side of the street and deposited it on the other with a whisper.

He shook his leg a couple of times to free it.

God it was hot here.

Hot enough to create a Death for each and every kind of creature that died out here.

Unfortunately, without flesh or skin, he couldn't squint in the face of the relentless sun, or sweat to cool down.

He threw back his hood and scratched his skull behind the ear hole with a bony finger.

How long before the Powers That Be gave him a nice, cool Summer uniform.

Something elegant in linen would be best.

Maybe a little tailored suit, with a smooth fitted silhouette.

And a modern, streamlined watch to match.

And really, would a small, lightweight penknife he could slip in a breast pocket be too much to ask for?

But Death was halfway grateful it wasn't winter.

A few years ago, he'd lost a couple of toes when the street was boggy with red mud. Luckily, they grew back, though it was goddamned painful at the time.

Perhaps an elegant Italian leather shoe would help, though Death supposed he'd lose a whole foot in the mud that way.

He grinned at the thought of what the human archaeologists might make of digging up an Italian loafer with a skeletal foot inside.

The ghost of a Cobb & Co carriage careened down the street, its four skeletal horses skidding around the corner, narrowly missing the hotel verandah Death stood opposite.

The old Chinese man sitting on the verandah, barely started. He tamped the tobacco in his long stem clay pipe and lit it, sucking a little to draw the smoke up.

Li Quan propped his feet on the guardrails, and balanced on the back legs of the chair, idly pushing himself backwards and letting himself fall forward as he puffed.

Death checked his hourglass again and wondered if he could get away with kicking the legs out from under Quan.

A sulphur-crested cockatoo landed on the roof behind him with a thud, "G'day mate," it said as it walked along the gutter to stand more or less beside, but a little to the left of Death, "how's it hanging?"

Death turned and thrust his scythe at the bird to shoo it away, but it just lifted its yellow crest and spread its wings as it reared back, then leaned forward, folding its wings and making itself comfortable.

"As you know full well Mooyi," he said to the cockatoo, "I don't have an "it" to hang."

"Ah mate, that's harsh that is."

Death jerked the scythe again, but the bird just looked at him.

Li Quan sucked his pipe as he rocked, popping in syncopation with the creaking of the chair.

"Hello cocky," he said.

"Squawk," the cockatoo replied.

Silence, aside fromthe music Quan was making fell on the street.

He was the last man left in the town, last person if you want to be particular.

Technically he worked for Cobb & Co, running the hotel and taking care of the horses, but it had been a long time since the town was on a regular coach run.

He still cleaned the stables every morning, and lit the lamp every night as dusk fell, because even if there wasn't a coach with passengers, a rider might come by with a bag of rice, or a box of tea, or a letter.

In between, he tended his fruit and vegetable plot and distilled his own alcohols with the produce.

Or meditated and read the sutras.

But mostly just sat, looking out at the wide brown land he lived on.

Death turned away and glared into the heat haze shimmering across the far end of the street.

The shimmer intensified, and two figures emerged from within it.

One was a man with the head of an ox, and the other a man with the face of a horse.

Both were richly dressed in bright Chinese silks, padded and embroidered with gold threads into soft armour.

They carried tridents and chains, and wore swords tucked in their belts.

Worst of all, they wore long boots.

No.

Actually, worser than worst of all, they had hanging things.

Death stepped into the street between them and Quan.

"Death, be gone," said Ox-Head, "this is not your soul to collect."

Horse-Face nodded once in the affirmative.

"This is a country that believes in me," Death replied, "they don't know who you are."

"This is our soul, we will collect it," said Ox-Head, "because it is possible."

"Argh," grunted Death, "did you not hear me? This is my place, and these people don't know who you are."

Ox-Head put a hand on his sword, "Li Quan knows who we are, he is waiting for us."

Death bashed his scythe handle on the ground as another cockatoo landed on the roof of the derelict General Store.

"G'day mateys," it said.

"G'day mate, said Mooyi."

"Hello Cocky," said Quan.

Death feinted with his scythe, the bird raised its crest, flapped its wings a couple of times and jumped a little further down the street towards the animal-headed creatures.

"There's no need to be nasty," it said, "I'm just being a bit social mate."

"How is this going?" said Horse-Face.

"Hot enough for you mate?" the bird asked in reply.

Horse-Face shook his head and shrugged one shoulder.

Another cockatoo landed nearby, "all good mate?"

And another further away, "'ow ya goin' mate?"

Death's bones creaked as he tensed up.

"You right mate?" another bird asked as it landed.

Death clenched his fist.

And took a step forward as he lunged at Ox-Head who leaned to the side to dodge the punch.

Horse-Face slapped the back of Death's skull as he fell between them.

Death twisted his torso and doubled back towards Horse-Face, catching him with a one-two punch to the chest as he passed.

Horse-Face bent forward, then staggered back, trying to stay upright.

Death curled, and flipped, and leapt feet first towards Ox-Head, landing one foot to the guts as Ox-Head used the other to try to leverage Death's body into a spin away.

Death's foot came away at the ankle, and he screamed in shock and pain, landing awkwardly.

He was so angry, he swept his scythe towards Ox-Head who blocked him with his trident.

Barely hampered by his missing foot, Death squared off with Ox-Head, scythe swooping only to be met by the trident time and time again.

Horse-Face had no quarrel with Death, so he took a step back to watch the fight.

Occasionally twitching as if he was fighting too.

Quan, oblivious to the spirit plane battle in the street, put down his pipe and walked into the street.

He pulled a handful of seed from his pocket as he approached the cockatoo flock. "Hello cocky," he said again.

A couple of birds flew closer, watching him carefully.

Mooyi landed on his shoulder and rubbed his cheek against Quan's.

"G'day mate," he said, and Quan laughed as he reached out to scratch the back of the bird's neck.

"G'day you too."

Quan spread the seed on the General Store balustrade for the birds to eat, then took an apple and a penknife from his other pocket and carved a piece off for Mooyi.

As Mooyi started nibbling it, he carved a piece for himself to eat as well.

As the spirit fight intensified, he leaned up against the verandah post and watched the birds eat.

"Pretty birdie," he said, and one or another cockatoo squawked back.

Ox-Head twisted away, Death kicked him in the back of the knee with the stump of his leg.

As Ox-Head fell, Death's scythe sliced through the air and severed Quan's soul from his body.

Mooyi squawked and flew to the roof as Quan's body fell to the ground startling the cockatoos.

The rest of the flock launched upwards, screeching, in all directions.

The soul collectors were fully immersed by the fight and didn't notice the commotion.

Quan looked down at his body slumped on the ground, and then became aware of the fight going on in front of him.

His eyes widened, and his spirit hands flew to his mouth.

Of course he recognised Ox-Head and Horse-Face as the guardians of Diyu, there to take him before the courts of Hell.

But he had no idea who the robed skeleton was or why it was trying to prevent his justice.

He was more afraid than he had ever been while alive.

What would happen to him if he wasn't judged and punished according to the requirements of the sutras?

As Quan shrank back, Horse-Face leapt to Ox-Head's defence.

Quan felt as though all his future lives were blowing away from him like the red dirt in the wind.

While he was prepared to take the punishment he deserved, all he wanted was to stay in this place where he'd been so happy.

He'd defied his parents and village, and stayed many long years after they'd demanded he return.

A hairy black hand touched his shoulder for a moment, and he was infused with calm.

Wordlessly, the creature invited him to join the other souls from this place, and he readily agreed.

One by one, the cockatoos landed on and around Quan's body, and quietly watched the fight.

As Death twisted out from under Horse-Face's sword, he noticed the body.

He allowed the Chinese soul collectors to dismember his skeleton, barely flinching before he pulled himself together.

"Did something happen to Quan?" Death asked.

"Yeah, nah," said Mooyi, "the Yowie took 'im."

"The Yowie?"

"Yeah mate, the Yowie."

"What is this Yowie to do with Li Quan?" asked Ox-Head.

"Ah well," said Mooyi shrugging, "youse made him mad."

"Mad?" asked Horse-Face.

"Yeah mate, mad."

"Mooyi," said Death through gritted teeth, "if you don't tell me what happened to Quan this instant, so help me, I'll take you to Hell and see you stay there."

"Nah mate, you can't do that, I don't belong to you."

"Mooyi."

"All right mate, no need to get your knickers in a knot."

The cockatoos fell about laughing, and Death poked his scythe at them.

"Nah mate, it's not very respectful, is it?"

"What is your respect for this?" asked Ox-Head.

"Well, all this fighting about jurisdictions in front of the soul."

"Jurisdiction?"

"Yeah mate, jurisdiction."

"Jur-is-dic-tion," said Horse-Face as if he didn't know what the word meant.

"Yeah mate, you can't be fighting about who a soul belongs to when it's standing right there watchin' ya."

"Watching?"

"Yeah mate, he was watchin' youse fight over him."

"I do not understand," said Ox-Head.

"It's really very simple," said Death, "while we were fighting, this Yowie stole Quan's soul out from under us."

"That's right mate."

Death rubbed his skull above his eye sockets with his right thumb and middle finger, "by what reason does this Yowie have the first claim?"

"Ah mate! How long 'ave ya been coming here and ya still have no idea have ya?"

Death scuffed a toe in the dirt.

"Yowie took the first soul from this place to live in the Land of the Sky People."

Ox-Head gently scratched the back of his head with one of the points of his trident, "Yowie brought Li Quan to the air?"

"Yeah mate."

"Can we let him come back?"

"Nah mate, he's gone now. Just like when you take 'em to Diyu."

"While I concede that perhaps Yowie has jurisdiction, I'm not clear on why he took Quan," said Death

"Because Quan wanted 'im to, mate."

"Wanted him to?"

"Yeah mate, said 'e belonged here mate."

"Once belonged to here?" asked Horse-Face.

"Yeah mate, said this was 'is place."

Ox-Head looked at Horse-Face, "King Yama is not happy."

Horse-Face nodded, "There will paperwork there because it doesn't exist here?"

"I should think so, mate."

"One thing's for sure," said Death, "we can't be going around letting souls decide what happens to them, can we?"

The Chinese soul collectors shook their heads.

"Higher than my pay grade," said Ox-Head, "but I will pass it back."

"Do," said Death, "I'll recommend treaty negotiations commence immediately," and winked out.

Ox-Head turned to Horse-Face, "maybe it will be fine, King Yama likes paperwork."

"Also hope so," Horse-Face replied.

The air shimmered around them, and they disappeared into the haze.

"Well, that went well, eh mate?" asked Mooyi.

"Sure did, mate. Fancy a snack?"

"Yeah, I reckon. Gum tree mate?"

"Sounds good mate, I'll race ya."

A flurry of wings stirred the air, and the flock took to the sky, calling out to each other as they flew.

Back on the ground, the dust settled and lay still.

THE END

# ABOUT THE AUTHOR

Alexandria Blaelock writes stories, some of them for *Ellery Queen's Mystery Magazine* and *Pulphouse Fiction Magazine.*

She's also written five self-help books applying business techniques to personal matters like getting dressed, cleaning house, and feeding your friends.

She lives in a forest because she enjoys birdsong, the scent of gum leaves and the sun on her face. When not telecommuting to parallel universes from her Melbourne based imagination, she watches K-dramas, talks to animals, and drinks Campari. At the same time.

Discover more at www.alexandriablaelock.com.